Buster's Naughty Tricks

ISBN 978-0-545-50185-9

12 11 10 9 8 7 6 5 4 3 2 1   12 13 14 15 16 17/0

Printed in the U.S.A.   40
First Scholastic printing, December 2012

Sue Mongredien

Kitten Club

Buster's Naughty Tricks

Scholastic Inc.

Meet the Kitten Club girls!

Amy
& Ginger

Mia
& Smokey

Molly
& Truffle

Ella
& Honey

Ruby
& Ziggy

Lily
& Buster

Chapter I

"Lily! Are you ready? We need to leave for Kitten Club in two minutes!"

Lily McCarthy jumped at the sound of her mom's voice. Oops! She'd completely lost track of time, practicing her audition piece in her bedroom. The school play was being cast on Monday, and Lily desperately wanted to get the best part.

"Coming!" she shouted. "I'll just say good-bye to Buster."

Buster was Lily's black kitten. He was almost five months old and absolutely adorable, but also very naughty. He liked sharpening his claws on the furniture, and jumping up onto the kitchen counters, where he wasn't allowed. He also had the bad habit of curling up and going to sleep in the worst possible places . . . like on Mom's best silk pajamas, or on top of the television with his tail dangling over the screen. The other day, he even dozed off in the fruit bowl, leaving black fur all over the apples.

"Buster," Lily called, "where are you?"

She heard a sleepy meow from Mom and Dad's bedroom and her heart sank. Oh, no. Buster wasn't supposed to go in there ever since he'd made holes in Mom's favorite pajamas. She hurried in and scanned the room. Bed, closet, chest of drawers, baby Jessica's crib . . . Uh-oh. Buster was in Jessica's crib, snuggled up with her pink teddy bear, and looking very pleased with himself.

"Buster!" Lily hissed. "What are you doing in there?"

"Lily, we need to go," her mom called from downstairs.

"One minute!" she yelled back. She reached an arm into the crib and quickly scooped up her kitten. He began rumbling with purrs, but Lily didn't feel quite so happy. There was black fur all over Jessica's mattress. Mom was going to be so mad!

"Oh, Buster," she said, taking him out of the room and shutting the door firmly behind her. "What am I going to do with you?"

Mom wasn't too pleased to hear about Buster's latest napping spot when Lily broke the news in the car on the way to Kitten Club.

"How did he get in there?" Mom said, frustrated. "I know I didn't leave the door open."

Lily swallowed, remembering how she'd gone in the bedroom earlier to borrow Mom's hairbrush. "I . . . I think I might have left it open," she said. "Sorry, Mom."

Her mom sighed as she parked outside Mia's house and turned off the engine. "We'll just have to keep a closer eye on what he's

doing, and where he is," she said, unbuckling her seat belt. "And we'll have to try extra hard to remember to keep bedroom doors shut, so that he can't sneak in, okay?"

Mom got out and walked around to open the car door for Lily. She looked tired, Lily thought, noticing the dark rings under her eyes. She knew her mom hadn't slept very well lately because Jessica was teething and had been crying a lot in the night. To make matters worse, Dad was working out of town for a few weeks, so he wasn't around to help out.

Lily got out of the car and gave her mom a hug. "Sorry," she said again. "I'll try harder to stop Buster from sleeping where he shouldn't, Mom, I promise."

Her mom hugged her back. "We'll both

try," she said.
"Have fun at
Kitten Club,
love. Molly's
mom's going
to pick you
up, okay?"

Lily waved
as her mom drove
away, then walked
quickly through the rain up to Mia's front
door. She knew her friends would be
sympathetic about Buster misbehaving.
Thank goodness for Kitten Club!

Chapter 2

"Hi, Lily," Mia said, letting her inside.
"Great news. Dad took my sisters over to
visit my aunt, so it's just us and Mom.
Hooray!"

"Yay!" said Lily, stepping into the
warm house. Mia had one older sister and
one younger sister, and neither of them
were very good at letting the Kitten Club

girls have their meetings in peace.

Lily followed Mia into the living room, where the other girls were already waiting. In total, there were six of them in Kitten Club—Lily, Mia, Molly, Ella, Amy, and Ruby. Their kittens were all brothers and sisters, and the girls had met when they'd chosen them at Chestnut Farm in the summer.

"Hi, guys," Lily said as she walked into the room. "And hello, Smokey," she added, seeing Mia's fluffy gray kitten curled up on Amy's lap.

"Hi, Lily," the others chorused, smiling back at her.

"How's Buster?" asked Molly.

Lily groaned theatrically and shook her head. "Adorable but naughty," she said.

"I had to throw him out of Jessica's crib just before coming here. Mom was so annoyed when I told her where I'd found him, I thought she was going to crash the car."

"Oops," Ruby said. "Ziggy fell asleep on one of my teddy bears yesterday. They looked so cute—like they were cuddling!"

Mia and Lily sat down with the others, then Mia opened up the Kitten Club scrapbook, which the girls filled in every week, and turned to the next free page. "Now that we're all here, let's do the roll call," she said. "Green Eyes?"

"Meow," Amy said, answering to her club nickname.

"Alley Cat?"

"Meow," said Molly.

"Glamour-Puss?"

"Meow," said Ruby.

"Scatterbrain?"

"Meow . . . prrrr," said Lily, rubbing her head against Ella's arm, just like a cat. Everybody giggled.

"Tomboy?"

"M-meow," Ella managed to get out, still laughing.

"And Witch Cat—that's me," Mia said, ticking herself off.

"I've got something for you all," Amy said when Mia had finished. She reached into a plastic bag next to her and pulled out a sheaf of paper. "It's our magazine—Mom printed copies for everyone!"

The other girls let out loud squeals of excitement, making Smokey jerk awake, his ears swiveling back in surprise. Then his eyes widened happily at the sight of the empty plastic bag on the floor, and he stood up, wiggled his bottom, and pounced on it.

The girls all roared with laughter as the bag—and Smokey—went skidding along the carpet. He gave a mew of alarm and leaped off, staring suspiciously at the bag.

"Oh, Smokey," Mia giggled. "You looked like you were sledding there. Are you practicing in case it snows?"

"Dad said today's weather forecast is for snow," Amy said excitedly. "I hope it's right! Anyway," she went on, handing out copies of *MEOW!*, the special Kitten Club magazine that they'd made, "have a look at these!"

Her friends opened their copies at once. They'd each contributed different things to the magazine—jokes, puzzles, news, and all sorts of other fun stuff.

"Oh, wow," Molly said, leafing through her copy. "It looks awesome. I'm going to keep this forever."

"I can't wait to show Ziggy that he's in print." Ruby smiled, turning to a page she'd written about her kitten, which included a photo of him. "Fame at last!"

"We've got to do another copy in the new year," Mia said happily, scooping Smokey onto her lap as she read. "This looks fabulous."

Once everyone had admired the magazine, the girls took turns sharing their news. "We're getting our Christmas tree tomorrow," Ella said, hugging her knees. "I can't wait. Although I'm wondering what Honey's going to think of it. She's probably going to climb up it, knowing her."

"I bet Buster will do the same," Lily said, rolling her eyes. "Can you imagine how excited the kittens will be with all those ornaments swinging from the branches? Buster will think it's an enormous toy, just for him."

"What are you getting your kittens for Christmas?" Amy asked. "I saw a really cute food bowl in town with paw prints painted around the side. I'm saving up my allowance to buy it for Ginger."

"I might get Truffle a red velvet collar," Molly said thoughtfully. "She'd look so cute in it—and Christmasy, too!"

"Ziggy's going to have smoked fish for his Christmas dinner," Ruby said. "It's his absolute favorite treat."

Mia glanced at Smokey, who had leaped off her lap and was chasing a marble across the room. "We don't celebrate Christmas, but I'm going to get Smokey a present anyway," she said. "Have you seen those toy hamsters that whiz around everywhere? He would love one of those to play with."

Mia's mom came into the room just then. "Girls, would you like to make cookies?" she asked. "I've got some special cookie cutters that I thought you might like. . . ." She held up two silver cookie cutters—one shaped like a cat's head, and one the shape of a cat sitting up.

"Yes, please!" Amy cried, getting to her feet at once.

"Ooh, yummy," the others echoed.

"Go and wash your hands, then, and meet me in the kitchen." Mia's mom smiled.

The girls didn't need to be told twice! Mia's mom helped them make the sugar cookie dough, and then they took turns rolling out a lump of it and cutting it into cat shapes.

While the cookies were baking, they cleaned up together. Mia scooped up some of the bubbles from the sink and blew them into the air for Smokey to chase. As Lily dried the cookie cutters, she told her friends about the school play she was planning to audition for. "It's called *The Christmas Angel*," she told them, and grinned. "Guess which part I'm hoping to get?"

"Could it be the Christmas Angel, by any chance?" Molly laughed.

"You guessed it," Lily said, high-fiving Molly. "I hope they pick me. It's the best part in the whole show—and the best costume, too. Sparkly wings and everything!" And then she was off, pretending to fly around the room, flapping her arms with a dreamy, angelic expression on her face. "Si-i-i-ilent night," she warbled. "Ho-o-o-oly night . . ."

The others burst into laughter. Even Mrs. Khaliq smiled at Lily's dramatics. "If anyone deserves to get the part, it's you, Lily," she said, taking a tray of sweet-smelling cookies from the oven. "But right now, I need you all to be kitchen angels and finish clearing up in here. Then, when these have cooled down, you can taste one. Do we have a deal?"

"Deal!" everyone chorused. Lily stopped flapping and smiled at her friends. She loved being in Kitten Club almost as much as she loved Christmas. And with Buster in the family now, she knew it was going to be the best Christmas ever.

Chapter 3

The next day, as soon as Lily woke up, she knew something was different. The light coming through the gap in her curtains looked strangely bright. She rolled out of bed —brrr, it was freezing—and pulled open the curtains . . . then squealed. It had snowed in the night, and the whole yard was covered in a thick white blanket!

"Mom! Mom!" she yelled, racing downstairs at full speed. "Have you seen the snow?"

Lily's mom was in the kitchen feeding Jessica her breakfast. Jessica bounced up and down in her high chair, beaming as her big sister burst into the room. "Yes, there's a lot of it, isn't there?" Mom said. "Have some breakfast, Lil, then we can bundle up and go outside."

Buster was sitting on the windowsill, staring out the window. He had a puzzled expression, as if he didn't understand what had happened to his yard. Lily picked him up and danced around with him. "Oh, Buster, you're going to love the snow—it's so much fun! We can make a snowman, Mom. We can even make a snow-cat!"

Lily's mom laughed at her excitement.
"Good idea," she said. "But how about
breakfast first? There's oatmeal on the stove
if you want something hot."

Buster didn't like being bounced around,
and he squirmed out of Lily's arms, plopping
down onto the table. Jessica shrieked in
excitement as he skidded on the slippery
surface. "Off the table!" Mom said to him,
her smile vanishing. "Go on, shoo!"

Lily sat down with Buster on her lap, telling him all the fun things they were going to do in the snow, while she gobbled up her breakfast. Then she went upstairs and put on three sweaters, a pair of leggings with snow pants over them, and two pairs of socks, before coming down again to add her coat, a wool hat, a scarf, gloves, and her rubber boots.

"Ready!" she declared, waddling awkwardly to the back door. She was so bulky with all her layers that moving around felt very strange! "Come on, Buster, let's play outside. Snow is the best!"

Unfortunately, it quickly became clear that Buster didn't share Lily's view that snow was

the best. As soon as Lily plopped him down on
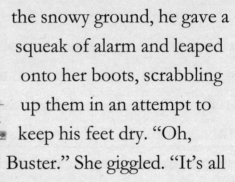
the snowy ground, he gave a
squeak of alarm and leaped
onto her boots, scrabbling
up them in an attempt to
keep his feet dry. "Oh,
Buster." She giggled. "It's all
right. It's fun! Try it out."

She peeled his paws off her boots and
set him down on the snow. Buster's legs
still weren't very long, so the snow came
right over his paws and almost up to his
soft tummy. He gazed up at Lily with big,
bewildered eyes, as if to say, *Why are you doing
this to me?*

Lily leaned down to pet him. "It's okay,
kitty," she said soothingly. "You'll get used to
it. Come on, let's make footprints."

But Buster put his nose
in the air and stalked off
toward the back door. He'd
had quite enough of the
cold, thank you very much.
He had to pick his feet up
extra high to walk through
the snow, leaving the cutest
little prints. Pieces of ice clung
to his belly, and he kept his tail
firmly up as if he was determined not to
get a single hair of it cold or wet.

Lily's mom came outside with Jessica
balanced on her hip, and they watched Buster
leap up the back step into the house and give
himself a good shake.

"He's as much of a drama queen as you
are," Mom joked.

Lily felt a little disappointed. "I wanted him to play with me, Mom," she said.

"Cats aren't big fans of snow," her mom said. "They don't like getting their paws wet."

"Oh, well," Lily said. "Maybe he'll be braver later on. Will you help me make a snow-cat, Mom? Let's make a really cute one." She grinned, seeing Buster watching them out of the window. "If we make a realistic-looking one, you never know, Buster might come out and try to make friends with it!"

"It was so much fun playing in the snow, Dad —I wish you'd been here with us," Lily said later that evening when he called.

"I wish I'd been there, too," her dad

replied. "If it's still snowy when I'm back at Christmas, we'll have the biggest and best snowball fight ever."

Lily smiled. She was curled up on the sofa in her pajamas, and had just gotten out of the bath. She half watched Buster chasing a ball around while she chatted. "You will be back for the school play, won't you?" she asked. "The auditions are tomorrow, and I'm trying out for the main part, you know."

"I'll do my best," Dad said, "but I can't promise anything right now."

Lily was distracted by Buster suddenly leaping onto the table and attacking a large potted plant. "I'd better go," she said, hurrying across the room as the bold kitten grabbed a dangling leaf with his paws and began swinging from it. "Bye, Dad."

"Good luck tomorrow," he said. "Bye,
Lils."

"Buster!" Lily hissed, trying to detach his
claws from the plant. He'd broken one of
its stems so that it drooped down forlornly.
"You're not allowed up there, you monkey,"
she told him, picking him up and kissing his
nose. "Come upstairs with me instead. You
can listen to me practice for my audition
again."

The next morning, Lily felt jittery as she got ready for school. It was Audition Day! She knew her lines perfectly, but hoped her mind didn't go blank when it was her turn to perform. "I wish I could take you to school with me, Buster," she said as she finished brushing her teeth. "I need a lucky mascot today."

Buster, who was in the bathroom with her, seemed more interested in the long piece of toilet paper dangling from the roll than in being a lucky mascot. He stretched up on his hind legs to reach it and almost fell over backward. Lily giggled as she washed her face. Buster, meanwhile, was still desperate to reach the toilet paper.

He leaped up even higher this time, a paw
outstretched, and managed to hook his claw
into the paper. As he landed
on the ground, the paper
unrolled after him, falling
in a heap on his head!
Lily burst out laughing
as Buster gave a surprised
squeak. He really was the
funniest kitten in the world! "We'd better
clean this up before Mom notices," she said,
still chuckling. "What a troublemaker!"

Buster gazed up at her, his beautiful green
eyes wide and innocent looking, as if to say, *Me?*
Trouble?

Lily couldn't help cuddling before she tidied
up. Troublemaker or not, she just couldn't resist
him.

The auditions took place at lunchtime.
Along with the part of the Christmas Angel,
there were also roles for Mary, Joseph, three
wise men, shepherds, a Christmas tree, a
modern-day family, and a whole host of
other angels who'd be singing as a choir.
Some of Lily's friends and classmates were
nervous about auditioning. Alice forgot her
lines and turned bright red. Willow looked
terrified and couldn't manage more than a
mumble. And Emily got all giggly and kept
putting her hand over her mouth like she
was embarrassed. Watching them made Lily
feel nervous, too. She wanted to be the angel
so bad!

When it was her turn, she stood up, took

a deep breath, and tried to imagine that
she was the angel. She thought about the
graceful way an angel would move, and
tried to copy that grace as she walked to
the center of the stage. She kept her head
up, looked right at the teachers, then
spoke clearly and confidently.

As the words came out, she really felt for a moment that she was the Christmas Angel, and that she could make everyone in the world have the most wonderful Christmas. Before she knew it, she'd reached the end of her lines—and everybody clapped.

"Very nice, Lily, thank you," said Mrs. Matthews, the drama teacher.

"You were awesome," Willow told her, her eyes shining, as she sat down again.

"You were great," Emily agreed.

"Thank you," Lily said. It had taken her a few seconds to remember that she was Lily McCarthy, and not actually the Christmas Angel. She crossed her fingers. "Let's hope the teachers thought so, too."

Chapter 4

"Molly, it's Lily. Guess what?"

"What?" said Molly through the phone.

"I got the part. I'm the Christmas Angel!"

"Oh, cool! That's awesome, Lily," Molly cried, sounding almost as excited as Lily felt.

Lily couldn't stop beaming. The cast list

had been put up at the end of the day, and she'd had to check it at least five times before she could believe it was real. But her name had been there in black and white: Christmas Angel—Lily McCarthy. YAY!

"I'm so pumped," she told Molly. "It's the biggest part by far—I've got tons of lines to learn." She petted Buster, who was climbing up her sweater, and giggled as his fluffy head tickled her neck. "The only bad thing is that I've got rehearsals almost every night," she went on, trying to unhook Buster's claws. "So I won't get to play with Buster as much after school. But it's only for a few weeks."

"He'll be all right," Molly said. "Hey, will your dad be back in time to see the show?"

Lily plopped Buster into her lap, but he scampered away and started sharpening his claws on the arm of the sofa. "No, Buster!" she yelped as a thread came loose. "Um . . . I don't know," she replied to Molly. "I hope so. He's not sure yet. Anyway, just wanted to tell you my good news. I'll see you on Saturday for Kitten Club, okay? I'd better run— Buster's in one of his crazy moods. Byeeee!"

By the time Saturday came around, Lily had already had three play rehearsals, and loved every minute of them. The story of the play was of the Christmas Angel watching over the world in December, and seeing a family that was constantly arguing. Over the course of the play, the Christmas Angel reminded the family members of the true meaning of Christmas, and inspired them to be kinder to one another. There were lots of songs to learn along with her lines, but Lily was really enjoying herself.

The only problem was that Buster seemed to be behaving extra badly in Lily's absence. Mom had caught him sharpening his claws on the table leg, which had left scratch marks in the wood. He'd knocked over a lamp in the living room by pouncing on the tassels that dangled so temptingly from the lampshade, and he'd actually lashed out at Jessica when she'd pulled him off the sofa by his tail. Jessica had howled with shock, apparently, and had a long red scratch on her arm to show for the encounter.

"Thank goodness it's the weekend now, and I can keep an eye on you," Lily told Buster as she tried on her angel costume in her bedroom. She beamed at her reflection. Mrs. Cookson, the teacher who was making the costumes for the play, had given Lily her outfit the day before at school. It was gorgeous! The dress was silver and sparkly and covered with sequins, and she also had the most wonderful glittering, gauzy wings edged with long white feathers.

Buster eyed Lily's wings with interest as she fastened them to her back, and stared as she pretended to fly around the room. "Silly billy, do you think I'm a bird?" Lily laughed when he chased after her.

"Lily!" called Mom just then from downstairs. "Can you watch Jessica for a minute while I sort this laundry?"

"Sure," Lily shouted back. She took off the dress and wings, and laid them carefully on her bed. The Kitten Club meeting was at her house today, and she couldn't wait to show the costume to her friends.

She grabbed Buster and took him down to the living room, where Jessica was sitting on the carpet, surrounded by toys. She was

playing with some stacking rings, and every time she put a ring onto the central pole, Lily would cheer and clap and do a little dance. Jessica thought this was the funniest thing ever and got more and more excited, laughing even before she'd put a ring onto the pole, in anticipation of Lily doing the dance. Meanwhile, Buster was careening around the room, chasing a pink squeaky ball.

Lily loved making Jessica laugh, and started thinking of other ways to amuse her. She put the stacking rings onto her head, then wobbled her head around until they plopped off, one by one. Jessica squealed and clapped at the sight. Then Lily juggled Jessica's squishy beanbags, making funny faces and pretending to fall over as she caught them. Jessica nearly fell over herself from laughing so much.

Jessica wasn't the only one who was watching Lily's antics now. Buster was fascinated by the flying beanbags, too, and sat staring at them, his little eyes tracking their movements. Then, as Lily threw one of the beanbags too far, Buster went sprinting after it and pounced on it. Jessica thought this was hilarious and laughed even harder.

Pleased that Buster wanted to join in the game, Lily started throwing the beanbags for him to pounce on. She was laughing so hard herself that her throws became wilder and wilder—and one beanbag flew right up onto the mantelpiece, where it just missed a glass vase. Buster didn't hesitate. He leaped onto the bookcase, and then onto the mantelpiece. But the mantelpiece was marble, which was slippery under his feet . . . so he skidded right along it, knocking everything off as he went!

Lily gasped in horror as the vase fell off and smashed, the framed photos of Lily and Jessica toppled over with a horrible shattering sound, and Mom's favorite stone paperweight in the shape of an eagle fell off and cracked right in half.

Jessica burst into shocked tears. "Oh, no," muttered Lily. Buster, sensing a scolding, hurtled down from the mantelpiece, his ears flattened in alarm.

"What on earth was that?" cried Mom, hurrying through from the kitchen just in time to see Buster streak out of the room and upstairs. She put a hand up to her mouth and 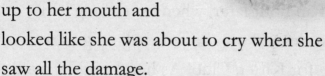 looked like she was about to cry when she saw all the damage.

"I'm sorry, Mom—it was my fault," Lily said. She felt awful.

"All my nice things," said Mom. "That cat, honestly—he's more trouble than he's worth!"

Chapter 5

Half an hour later, when everything had
been cleaned up, the doorbell rang. It was
time for Kitten Club! As her friends arrived,
Lily led them through to the kitchen, where
she'd set out a plate of snacks and some
glasses of lemonade. She couldn't really relax
for the first few minutes, though. All she
could think of was Mom saying that Buster

was more trouble than he was worth. She'd said it as if she really hated him!

"Are you okay, Lily?" Molly asked, nudging her after a while. "You're very quiet."

"Yeah, that's not like you, Lils," Ella added, leaning forward. "What's up? And where's Buster, anyway?"

Lily sighed. "Hiding upstairs from Mom, probably," she said. "He's in *huuuge* trouble right now." She went on to explain what had just happened.

"All kittens break stuff," Amy said kindly. "They can't help it. Ginger knocked over a potted plant on our porch last week, and the pot smashed. It was only an accident, so we couldn't be too angry."

"I know, but the problem is, Buster just

keeps doing these things," Lily replied.
"Like, he's wrecked the furniture and Mom's
pajamas, and smashed her vase and
paperweight. . . . She's getting really fed up
with him. Today she even said she thought
he was more trouble than he was worth—like
she'd rather not have him at all!"

Everyone got quiet at this. "People say
things like that when they're angry, but they
don't always mean it," Ruby said.

Lily shrugged. "You didn't see
her face," she said gloomily.
"She was like this—"
And Lily made the most
shocked, horrified,
furious expression she
could muster, which made
the others laugh.

"You are so going to be an actress, Lily," Mia said, spluttering on her lemonade. "Hey, that reminds me, how did your audition go?"

Lily smiled for what felt like the first time in a long time. "I got the part!" she said. "I'm the Christmas Angel. Oh, and wait till you see my dress—it's amazing." She stood up, remembering it was upstairs on her bed. "Actually . . . why don't you come and have a look? We can also see what Buster's up to and make sure he's not causing any more trouble."

The girls followed Lily upstairs. As she reached her bedroom, she pushed open the door and said, "Ta-da!" But the smile vanished from her face as she realized that Buster was on her bed, having some kind of

fight with her dress. The wings were ripped,
sequins and feathers had been torn off, and
he was kicking and chewing at the neckline.
It was ruined!

Lily let out a scream. "Buster! Oh, Buster,
how could you?" she wailed.

Buster, realizing he was in trouble again,
leaped off the bed in a panic, feathers

floating after him, and scurried out of the room, almost tripping in his haste to get away.

The girls crowded in to inspect the damage. "It's completely wrecked," Lily said, bursting into tears. "Mrs. Cookson's going to go nuts when she sees it. And what will Mom say?"

"What will Mom say about what?" came a voice. Then Lily's mom gasped as she saw what had happened. "Oh, no. Your dress!"

Tears rolled down Lily's face. "I must have left my bedroom door open earlier," she said miserably. "It's all my fault—again!"

Ella and Ruby, who were next to Lily, both put an arm around her and tried to comfort her. It was awful seeing bubbly Lily

so miserable. "We can fix it," Ruby said, handing her friend a tissue. "My mom's amazing with a sewing machine. I bet she wouldn't mind repairing the wings."

"We can stick the

feathers back on, too," Molly put in. "My dad has some superglue—I'm sure he'll help us."

"I'll see if I can patch up the dress later." Mom sighed, looking thoroughly fed up. "I've got to go feed Jessica now, though."

Lily's mom left the room and the girls crowded around Lily.

"Don't worry, we'll figure it out," Amy said, picking up some of the feathers.

Lily blew her nose and gave her friends a watery smile. "Thanks, guys," she said. "I shouldn't have shouted at Buster like that— he didn't know it was my special costume. I should have hung it up somewhere safe where he couldn't reach it, and shut my door, but I forgot. It's—"

She broke off as they heard Lily's mom

scolding Buster downstairs. "No! Bad! Claws OFF, Buster. Honestly! If I'd known just how much trouble you were going to be, I'd never have let Lily get you in the first place."

Lily's mouth dropped open in horror, and she looked as if she was about to cry again. "Did you hear that?" She gulped. "I *have* to make Buster behave better. What if Mom decides she's had enough of his naughty tricks and wants to give him away?"

"She won't," Molly said immediately, helping Amy pick up the last few feathers. "No way. Your mom wouldn't do that."

"But she just said she wishes we'd never gotten him," Lily sniffled. Her tummy ached at the thought of not having Buster. She couldn't bear to even imagine it. "He keeps breaking things and scratching the furniture—he's driving her crazy."

"Maybe Buster needs a scratching post to stop him from sharpening his claws on everything else," Mia suggested. "You can buy them in pet stores. While it's cold and rainy and the kittens don't want to go outside, it might be good to have a scratching post in the house."

"Dad was talking about helping me make one," Ella put in. "Hey, I know! Why don't I ask if he'll help us all make scratching posts for our kittens the next time we have a Kitten Club meeting at my house?"

"Great idea," Ruby said. "And we could give them to the kittens as Christmas presents!"

Everyone liked the sound of that—especially Lily. "I need to try harder, too," she said, rubbing her red eyes with the tissue. "I have to remember to close the bedroom and bathroom doors, and to get him to play outside more often." She gave her friends another watery smile. "In fact, why don't we take him into the yard now? Come on. We can give him his first Kitten Training lesson."

Chapter 6

The girls bundled up in their coats and scarves and took Buster into the yard. "A scratching post is a great idea," Lily said, "but I'm not sure I can wait until Christmas. Let's see if we can teach him to sharpen his claws outside for now—on tree trunks or on the fence or . . . well, on anything, as long as it isn't furniture!"

They walked over to the cherry tree, and Lily crouched down in front of it, still holding her kitten. "Here we are," she said. "Now, this is what you need to do. . . ." She put Buster's front paws on the tree in the perfect trunk-scratching position. But Buster wriggled out of her grasp and went off to sniff a nearby stone.

"Buster! Pay attention," Molly said.

"Watch me, Buster," Lily said. She put her hands on the trunk, pretending to be a cat as she scraped her fingers down the bark. "See? Easy. Now it's your turn."

Again, she picked him up and set his front paws against the bark. "Sharpen your claws," she told him. "Come on!"

"It's much better than furniture," Mia said encouragingly. "Give it a try, Buster."

But either Buster didn't understand or he just wasn't interested in doing what he was told. Instead, he scampered off to pounce on some long blades of grass that were blowing in the wind.

Lily sighed. "We'll try again tomorrow," she said, feeling a little downcast. "But really, Buster, you need to scratch out here. You have to get yourself back into Mom's good graces, otherwise . . ." She winced, not wanting to think about what might happen. Her mom's words about wishing she'd never

agreed to a kitten kept running through her head. Lily had to help him become better behaved.

Just then Buster did a flying leap right into the rosemary plant and started chewing its stems. Lily groaned and clapped a hand to her head. "It'll take more than a quick lesson in the yard to stop his crazy behavior, that's for sure." She sighed.

The girls played with Buster outside for a while longer. Ella suggested that lots of outdoor play might tire him out, so he'd sleep more indoors and wouldn't have time to cause trouble. "Good thinking," Lily said, and shivered. "*Brrrr*. Let's go in now, though, and warm up. I'm cold!"

Lily's mom had left out some art supplies for the girls—different colors of paper, pens,

pencils, glitter, and glue—and they sat around the kitchen table with mugs of hot chocolate, making Christmas cards for their kittens. Lily drew a picture of herself as the Christmas Angel next to Buster with a matching silver halo above his head. "I'll help him to be a little angel from now on," she vowed, adding smiles to both of their faces. She glanced over at Buster. He was now fast asleep in his basket, worn out after his outdoor adventures—just as Ella had predicted.

"He looks so adorable when he's asleep," Amy said, seeing Lily gazing at him.

Lily smiled. "Doesn't he? Good as gold. You'd never guess it was the same kitten who wrecked my dress earlier."

"Speaking of which . . ." Lily's mom said as she came into the room. She was carrying the remains of Lily's costume along with a flower-girl dress Lily had worn the previous summer, which was now a little too small for her. "I think I'll be able to repair your angel dress using the fabric from this," she said. "Will that be all right?"

Lily was so relieved her mom didn't sound angry anymore that she ran over and hugged her. "Thanks, Mom," she said. "That sounds perfect."

During the next week, the rehearsals for the Christmas play took place every day after school. Lily was really enjoying learning her part, aside from the fact that she saw less of Buster. Unfortunately, this meant less time for her Kitten Training and her plans to tire him out in the yard, especially since it was dark by the time she got home.

Meanwhile, Buster seemed to be getting naughtier and naughtier.

On Monday, he jumped onto the breakfast table and knocked over Lily's glass of milk. On Tuesday, he clawed huge scratches in the side of the sofa. And on Wednesday, he chewed through the electric cord of a lamp, dug all the soil out of one

of the houseplants, and bit Jessica when she pulled his tail!

By Thursday, Lily was dreading going home to see what awful things Buster had done, and found it really hard to concentrate on the play rehearsal. Mom had looked utterly exasperated with Buster's antics the night before, and Lily was more convinced than ever that she was having second thoughts about having such a naughty pet.

After the rehearsal that evening, one of Lily's friend's moms gave her a ride home. As soon as she got in the house, she pulled her coat off and called Buster's name.

"Ahh," her mom said. "Lily—I need to talk to you about Buster. . . ."

But Lily was already in the kitchen, and stopped dead in her tracks when she saw that

Buster's food bowl and cat bed had vanished.
I need to talk to you about Buster, Mom had said,
and immediately Lily feared the worst.

Could Mom have already gotten rid of him?

Chapter 7

Lily couldn't help herself. She burst into a flood of tears at the thought of never seeing her funny, adorable kitten again. This was going to be the worst Christmas ever! Why hadn't she tried harder to train him? Why hadn't she done a better job of keeping him amused so that he wouldn't do naughty things? This was all her fault!

"Lily, what's the matter?" her mom said, coming into the kitchen just then and finding Lily in a sobbing heap on the floor.

"Oh, Mom, why did you have to give Buster away?" Lily wailed. "I never even got to say good-bye!"

"Lily McCarthy, what are you talking about?" Mom asked, crouching beside her and putting an arm around her. "Buster hasn't gone anywhere—he's fast asleep on the sofa."

Lily sniffed and stared at Mom. "He's . . . on the sofa?" she hiccuped. "You haven't given him away?"

"Of course I haven't given him away,"

Mom exclaimed, ruffling Lily's hair. "I wouldn't dream of it! Yes, he's been a bit of a pest recently, but he's only a kitten. He'll be calmer when he's older." She chuckled. "Just like you and Jessica. Believe me, Lils, you were much more trouble than any kitten when you were a toddler. But it never crossed my mind to give *you* to anyone else."

Lily blew her nose and dabbed at her eyes. "When Buster's bowl and bed weren't there, I just thought . . . " she said, relief flooding through her. "Since you've been so annoyed with him this week, I've been so worried. I thought you didn't want us to have a kitten anymore."

Her mom hugged her. "Buster's bowl is in the dishwasher," she said. "And his bed is in the laundry room, where I gave it a wash earlier. I know I've been a little bad-tempered lately, but it's just because I'm tired. That's what I was going to say when you came in—that I'm sorry for being grumpy with you and Buster. As soon as Jessica gets her new tooth, we should all sleep better, and I won't feel so frazzled." She kissed the top of Lily's head. "So you dry your eyes now and go and give that kitten of yours a big cuddle, because he's not going anywhere, okay?"

Lily nodded, feeling much better.

"Thanks, Mom," she said. "You're the best mom ever."

The next Saturday, the Kitten Club meeting was at Ella's house. True to her word, she'd asked her dad if they could make kitten

scratching posts, and he'd gathered some short planks of wood and a roll of sisal—thin, hairy rope—that they could use.

Ella's dad cut lengths of sisal for them and nailed one end of each piece to the tops of their wooden boards.

"Now you need to wind the rope around and around the board, keeping the loops tightly together," he told them. "When you're done, I'll nail the other end down, too, and then we'll attach the boards to their bases."

The girls began winding the rough rope around their pieces of wood. Once they'd finished, and Ella's dad had nailed each rope end in place and fastened the boards to their wooden bases, Ella's mom produced a bag of ribbons and plastic ornaments. She suggested that the girls attach some to the tops of the scratching posts.

"Along with making them look pretty, it'll encourage the kittens to reach up and grab them—and hopefully they'll quickly learn that the rope is really good to sharpen their claws on," she said.

"Or you can tie catnip toys to the top," Ella's dad suggested. "They love the smell of that."

The girls chatted while they made their posts. "This is going to be Buster's New Year's resolution," Lily decided. "To learn to use his scratching post so that he stops sharpening his claws on the furniture."

"Truffle's resolution should be to grow up into a big brave cat, who doesn't put up with any nonsense from my brothers or dog." Molly laughed. "Although she is getting feistier already. The other day my brother Luke was playing a really noisy game on the PlayStation, and Truffle managed to turn off the TV by jumping onto the remote. It was so funny! It was just an accident, but you should have seen

Luke's face. The Kitten Strikes Back!"

"Honey's resolution is to chill out a little," Ella said, tying a long silver ribbon with a jingling bell on the end to her scratching post. But the moment the words were out of her mouth, she let out a shriek as Honey suddenly came flying through the air onto her lap, making everyone jump.

The girls all laughed. "I think Honey's got other ideas about your resolution for her." Ruby chuckled. "Chilling out is boring, right, Honey?"

"I can't wait for Christmas," Amy said, putting the finishing touches on her

scratching post. "I'm going to hang up a stocking for Ginger, just in case 'Santa Paws' stops by with some little treats."

"Great idea," Lily said. "Ooh, and speaking of Christmas, I got you all tickets to see me in my school play next Friday night. Mom said we could have a little party back at our house afterward with hot chocolate and cookies."

"And can we get your autograph for when you're really famous?" Molly joked. "We can tell everyone that we saw you in your first starring role!"

Lily struck a dramatic pose, and the others laughed. Then Honey leaped onto the table and skidded right through a tangle of ribbons. "Oh, Honey." Ella giggled, unraveling the wild-eyed kitten. "Were you trying to wrap yourself up as an early present? You'd be the best Christmas present ever!"

Once Lily was home that afternoon, she decided that she'd give Buster his Christmas present early. There was no time to lose!

She already knew he loved the smell of catnip since he had a catnip mouse that he often played with, so she tied its tail onto one of the ribbons at the top of the scratching post. Then she put it down on the kitchen floor and brought him over to show him his new present.

Buster was intrigued by the ribbons and toys at the top of the post, and reached up his soft paws to get them. Lily could see his

little black nose twitching, too, as he smelled the catnip. And then, as his claws caught in the rope, he pulled his paw free and began scratching it in earnest.

"Oh, good boy, Buster," Lily said, petting him.

Buster immediately froze and looked guilty —as if he thought Lily was about to scold him for sharpening his claws.

Lily smiled. "You keep on scratching, mister," she told him, tickling him under the chin until he began to purr. "This is the one place in the whole house that you're allowed to sharpen your claws, okay?"

Buster purred even louder, and Lily felt like purring, too, when he kept on scratching at the sisal-covered post for several minutes. "There, doesn't that feel nice?" she cooed, petting him happily. "Now we just need you to stop climbing shelves and knocking things off and doing anything else naughty," she went on. "And everything will be perfect. Okay?"

Chapter 8

The next week seemed to fly by. The good news was that the weather was much nicer, so Buster spent a lot of the day outside and less time inside wrecking the house, according to Mom. He'd also gotten the hang of his scratching post, and loved sharpening his claws on it.

The bad news was that Lily's dad still

wasn't sure if he'd be back in town in time to see the play. "I'm sorry, love," he said on the phone the night before the show. "I'll do my best to get there and see you, but I just can't promise it."

"Don't worry, Dad, I understand," Lily managed to say, although there was a big lump in her throat. She was gladder than ever that her Kitten Club friends would be in the audience to watch her.

The next day, Lily had butterflies in her tummy like never before. They'd had a dress rehearsal that morning in front of the rest of the school, and all sorts of things had gone wrong—one of the children who was dressed

up as a Christmas tree had tripped and hurt
herself onstage, the snowman had forgotten
his lines, and the baby Jesus doll had fallen
out of the crib with a loud clatter. Worst of
all, when Lily came out to say her first lines,
her mind went completely blank. "Good
evening to you all," she heard Mrs. Matthews
whisper from the side of the stage, and then,
thankfully, the words fell back into her head.
"Good evening to you all," she repeated. "I
am the Christmas Angel, come to Earth . . ."

"Oh, dear," one of the older girls had
said once the curtain had fallen and the dress
rehearsal was over. "That didn't go very well."

Mrs. Matthews didn't look too
concerned. "That's what dress rehearsals
are for, though," she said confidently.
"You'll see. It'll be all right tonight."

When the time came to put on her costume that evening, Lily could hardly pull up her silver tights because her hands were shaking so much. Luckily, Mom had been able to repair her dress pretty well with the extra flower-girl dress fabric, and the wings had been patched up, too. Once she was dressed and in her wings and halo, Mrs. Matthews patted on some sparkly face powder with a powder puff, and added a few silver sprinkles above her eyes. She was ready!

Backstage, Lily and the other actors could hear the auditorium filling up with parents and friends. Some of the performers were getting giddy with nerves while others wanted to sit very still by themselves. Lily's heart was pounding, she needed to use the bathroom, and her hands felt clammy. Oh, why had she tried out for the Christmas Angel? She was going to forget all her lines again and make a complete idiot of herself! She wished she could be safely at home with Buster right now.

"Special delivery for Lily McCarthy," came a voice just then, and Lily swung around in delight. She'd recognize that voice anywhere —her dad! She flung her arms around him and hugged him so tightly she could hardly breathe.

"You made it!" she cried happily. "Oh, Dad, I've really missed you!"

He hugged her back, and she felt safe and warm in his arms, as if nothing could go wrong. "I've missed you, too, love," he said. "I'm so glad I made it home in time to see the show. Oh, and your friends wanted me to deliver this to you."

He gave her a handmade card with a black cat on the front. The words GOOD LUCK! were written above it, in Molly's handwriting. Smiling, Lily opened the card to see good-luck messages from all the Kitten Club girls — and even some paw prints—as if Buster was wishing her luck, too. Seeing her dad and the card made her feel a hundred times better. All of a sudden, she couldn't wait to get onstage.

"Is everyone ready?" Mrs. Matthews called just then, bustling into the backstage area. She raised her eyebrows at the sight of Lily's dad there. "Would you mind taking your seat now, Mr. McCarthy? The show's about to begin."

"Sure," he said, giving Lily's hand a last squeeze. "Good luck, Lils. See you later!"

"Bye, Dad." Lily smiled.

Suddenly, the auditorium got quiet. "Good evening, ladies and gentlemen, boys and girls," she heard the principal, Mr. Holmes, say. "Welcome to our school. We are proud to present to you our Christmas play, called *The Christmas Angel*."

Lily could hear the audience clapping, and

an icy chill trickled down her back. She took
a deep breath and walked out onto the stage,
her heart pounding. This was it—her big
moment in the spotlight!

"You were awesome, Lily," Molly said,
biting into a cookie and licking frosting off
her fingers. "The best actor in the whole
play."

"Really?" Lily blushed. "Honestly?"

"Really, honestly, truly," Molly assured
her. "You rocked!"

"She's right," Lily's dad said, hugging her
again. "You stole the show. I'm so proud of
you."

"What a star," Mom agreed with a wink.
"You were wonderful."

Lily and the other Kitten Club girls were back at Lily's house with steaming mugs of hot chocolate and whipped cream, and lots of cookies. The Christmas show had been amazing, even if Lily said so herself. She had loved being onstage and seeing her friends and family smiling back at her from the audience. And the roar of applause that had come at the end . . . it gave her goose bumps every time she thought about it.

"I can't believe it's all over," Lily said now, sipping her hot chocolate. "But next we have Christmas to look forward to!"

Her eye was caught by the Christmas tree in the corner of the room, which she and her mom had decorated with tinsel, ornaments, and strings of lights a few evenings earlier.

They'd decided to make it kitten-proof and baby-proof by not hanging anything on low branches. That way, neither Jessica nor Buster would be tempted to pull the decorations off.

"What does Buster think of your tree?" Ruby asked, seeing Lily looking at it. "Ziggy loves the lights on ours. We've got the kind that flash on and off, and he just sits there, in a trance, staring up at them."

"Buster's been pretty cool," Lily said. "He likes playing with the lower branches, jumping up and batting them, but that's about it. I think he might be growing up at last. He's definitely calmed down lately."

As if he'd heard the girls talking about him, Buster chose that very minute to scamper into the room. His ears were back, he had a wild look in his eyes, and he seemed to be in a mischievous mood. "Uh-oh, you spoke too soon." Ella laughed. "He's lively tonight. Getting excited about Christmas, huh, Buster?"

Buster certainly did seem excited about something. Lily took a piece of tinsel off the tree and dragged it around the room, and he chased after it at full tilt. Then he looked up at the Christmas tree and seemed to notice all the other decorations and tinsel on the higher branches. And before anyone could stop him, he'd leaped onto the mantelpiece and then

made a mighty jump from there to the top
branches of the tree.

"Buster! Oh, Buster, what are you doing?"
Lily cried, clapping a hand to her mouth.

Buster wrestled with a piece of tinsel
and sent a shiny red ornament flying off its
branch as he clambered frantically up the
tree. Then as he got higher up, he managed
to knock the gold cardboard star off the top
branch, sending it plunging
to the ground.

"He says he's the only Christmas star in this house, thank you very much." Molly chuckled. "Oh, Buster, you bad kitty!"

Lily was laughing so hard, she could barely stand up straight. "Come here, you crazy boy," she said, reaching up and pulling Buster out of the tree. "What are you doing? Just when I was telling everyone how calm you are, too!"

Buster purred in her arms, his green eyes reflecting the twinkling tree lights, and Lily laughed again and held him tight. "You are my Christmas star, Buster, don't worry," she told him. "And I just know all six of us girls and our purr-fect pets are going to have a very happy *mew* year!"

Don't miss:

Sue Mongredien

Kitten Club

Honey's New Friend

SCHOLASTIC